"Poo poo, bum bum, wee wee,"

I sing it all day long!

I used to

poo poo
wee wee

in my nappy every day.

But now I'm big and wearing pants –
it's toilet time . . .

HOORAY!

I sing it in the morning
when I feel I need a **wee**.

I climb upon my toilet throne like bathroom royalty!

I shout out,

"Poo poo, wee wee!"

when it's time for me to go.

I pull my pants down, then relax and let the **wee wee** flow.

Poo poo, bum bum, wee wee!

I sing my toilet song.

Poo poo, bum bum, wee wee!

I sing it all day long!

I sing it when I need a **poo.**
I feel it in my belly.

I wave bye-bye as poo plops down,

all brown and rather smelly.

After **poo poo wee wee,**
it's time to wipe my bum.

Because I'm still quite little,
I get help from Dad or Mum.

I take some toilet paper,
and I reach behind my back.

I drop it in the toilet bowl
to show I have the knack.

"Poo poo,
bum bum,
wee wee!"

I flush it all away.

It *whooshes*

down the toilet . . .

Where it goes, I cannot say.

Now my toilet job is done,

I pull my pants up high.

I wash my hands,
then dry them off

and wave the loo goodbye!

"Poo poo, bum bum,
wee wee,"

I sing my toilet song.

"Poo poo, bum bum, wee wee,"

I sing it all day long!

"Poo poo,
bum bum,
wee wee,"

we sing our
toilet song.

Look out for more Ladybird picture books . . .

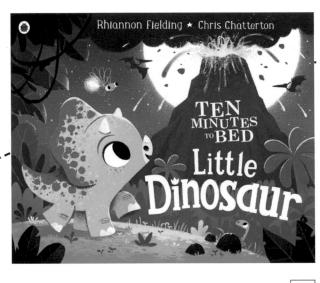

ISBN: 9780241348925

ISBN: 9780241386736

ISBN: 9780241464373

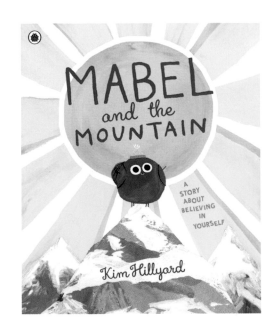

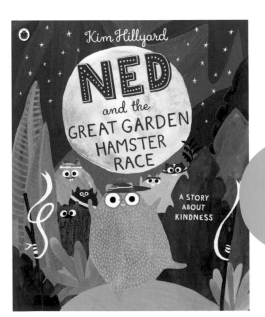

ISBN: 9780241407929

ISBN: 9780241413418

Can you collect them all?

POO POO BUM BUM WEE WEE

Written by
Steven Cowell

Illustrated by
Erica Salcedo

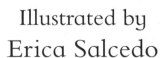

"Poo poo, bum bum, wee wee,"

I sing my toilet song.